THE STORY OF THE NUTCRACKER
Coloring Book

Adapted from the Story by
E. T. A. Hoffmann

Illustrated by
Thea Kliros

Dover Publications, Inc.
New York

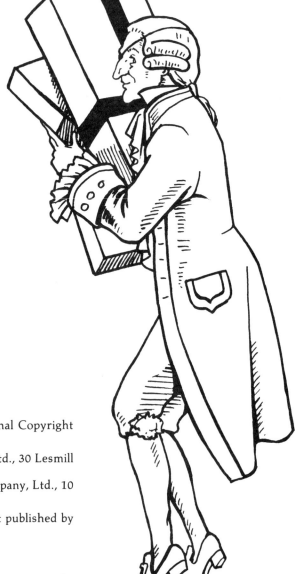

Published in Canada by General Publishing Company, Ltd., 30 Lesmill Road, Don Mills, Toronto, Ontario.
Published in the United Kingdom by Constable and Company, Ltd., 10 Orange Street, London WC2H 7EG.

The Story of the Nutcracker Coloring Book is a new work, first published by Dover Publications, Inc., in 1990.

DOVER *Pictorial Archive* SERIES

International Standard Book Number: 0-486-26405-X

Manufactured in the United States of America
Dover Publications, Inc., 31 East 2nd Street, Mineola, N.Y. 11501

Nutcracker and the King of the Mice

O N DECEMBER 24, the children of Dr. and Mrs. Stahlbaum were not allowed to enter the drawing room. Fritz and Marie had to wait, huddled together, in the small parlor, while from the drawing room they could hear the rattling and hammering that had been going on all day. In the evening, as it grew darker, the children began to feel creepy. Only a short time before, Godpapa Drosselmeier, a wiry little man with a patch over one eye, a yellow coat and a glass wig (for he was quite bald), had slipped into the drawing room with packages under his arms.

Godpapa Drosselmeier, a city councillor, knew all about clocks and mechanical toys. Each year he gave the children wonderful toys, and Marie and Fritz wondered what he had brought with him this year.

They did not have to wait long, for a bell rang and the doors to the

drawing room were thrown open and the children were allowed to enter. Bright lights shone everywhere and, at the center of the room, was a great Christmas tree. On a table in front of it were all sorts of presents—toy soldiers, picture books, toys, games and dolls.

Then another bell rang, and the children were taken to see a toy that Godpapa Drosselmeier had brought for Dr. and Mrs. Stahlbaum—a wonderful castle with mechanical people who moved up and down and through the castle's many rooms. But Fritz and Marie soon tired of the castle, and went back to their own toys.

When they had returned to their presents, Marie noticed one of Godpapa's gifts that she had overlooked in her excitement. It was a nutcracker dressed as a hussar with a little tin cap, and Marie fell in love with it immediately. Godpapa Drosselmeier showed Marie and Fritz how to pick up the nutcracker, put a nut into its mouth, close the lever and—CRACK!—the nut's shell had been broken so the children could eat the tasty kernel. Marie cracked nut after nut, until Fritz, always impatient, grabbed the nutcracker roughly, stuck the biggest, hardest nut he could find into its mouth and pushed down on the lever with all of his strength. CRACK! CRACK! Three little teeth fell out of the poor nutcracker's mouth.

Marie burst into tears, and took Nutcracker into her arms. She bound up his jaw with her handkerchief and held him very tenderly the whole evening, as she played with her other toys and looked through her new picture books. It grew very late. Fritz went to bed after Godpapa Drosselmeier left. Marie asked her mother if she could stay up a bit longer with her new toys, and her mother agreed, but before she left, she put out all the candles, leaving only a lamp burning.

Marie looked at Nutcracker. He was very pale. "Oh, little Nut-cracker," she said, "Don't be angry with Fritz. As for your teeth, Godpapa Drosselmeier should soon be able to fix them." As soon as Marie mentioned Drosselmeier's name, Nutcracker made a horrible face, and a green sparkle seemed to leap from his eyes. At first Marie was afraid, but then she told herself that it must have been the flickering light from the lamp, for the Nutcracker was a dear little thing, and she loved him.

Going to the cupboard in which the children's toys were kept, Marie took a little bed on which her newest doll, Miss Clara, was reclining. "Pardon me, Miss Clara, if I ask you to give up your bed to our poor, wounded Nutcracker." Nutcracker was put into the bed and tucked under the coverlets. Miss Clara, rather cross, had to make do with the dolls' sofa. Marie closed the cupboard, and was about to leave for bed, when—listen!—there came, at first softly, a whisper and a rustle from all over—behind the stove, under the chair and behind the cupboards. The clock on the wall began to whirr, louder and louder, but it would not strike the hour. Marie became afraid, and turned her back to leave the room, but noticed that, on top of the clock, in place of the carved owl, was Godpapa Drosselmeier, his coattails hanging down both sides of the clock, like wings.

"Godpapa, what are you doing up there?" cried Marie. But before she could say any more, there began a wild scurrying and squeaking, as though thousands of little feet were skittering to and fro behind the walls, in the ceiling and under the floor. Marie thought she saw thousands of little lights, but quickly realized they were tiny eyes shining out at her from the shadows—the eyes of an army of mice.

Before Marie had a chance to move, the floor burst open at her feet and there emerged a mouse with seven heads, each of them crowned. All the heads were hissing and squeaking orders to the mouse army to move to attack the toys in the cupboard. Marie backed away and, half fainting, leaned against the cupboard. Crash! Her elbow went through one of the panes of glass, and was cut. But Marie did not have time to tend to her wound, for a stirring was beginning inside the cupboard as the toys on the shelves began to move about. Little voices called to one another: "Awaken, awaken! Let all arms be taken! For this is the night of the terrible fight!" And indeed, as Marie watched, she saw, in a growing light that came from within the cupboard, all the dolls and toy soldiers running about in confusion, taking up weapons where they could find them. Suddenly, Nutcracker threw back the covers from his little bed and leapt up, shouting, "Crack, crack, crack! Stupid mousey pack. On to the attack! Crack, crack, crack! Stupid mousey pack!" In his excitement, he jumped from the high shelf and certainly would have been broken had not Marie caught him in her arms and put him gently on the floor. He knelt before her and told her that he was forever in her debt.

When he rose to his feet, he began to make preparations for the battle with the mice. Running about as fast as his little legs would carry him, he mobilized Fritz's tin soldiers and pressed various dolls into service to man cannon and bring gingerbread and nuts as ammunition.

The battle was fierce; the noise terrible. Miss Gertrude, one of Marie's oldest dolls, was seen running across the battlefield, crying, "Did I take such good care of myself for so many years only to perish miserably under my own roof?"

At first, things went well for Nutcracker. But reinforcements of mice streaming out of a chest of drawers soon turned the tide, and Nutcracker

suffered great losses, until he shouted in despair, "A horse! A horse! My kingdom for a horse!" With a horrible war cry, the King of the Mice went after Nutcracker, and would certainly have killed him had not Marie taken a slipper off her foot and thrown it at him with all her might.

At once, everything vanished. Marie felt the pain in her arm where she had been cut, and fainted.

When Marie awoke, she found herself in her own little bed, surrounded by her mother, her father and Godpapa Drosselmeier.

"Mother," asked Marie softly, "are the nasty mice gone now? And is Nutcracker safe?" Her mother stared at her. "What are you talking about, and what does Nutcracker have to do with mice?" Marie told her the strange events of the previous evening. "Nonsense," Mrs. Stahlbaum said. "It's my own fault for having let you stay up so late. You were tired, fell against the cupboard, cut yourself and fainted. If I hadn't come to fetch you, you might have bled to death. As it is, you're going to have to stay in bed for a while. Don't worry about Nutcracker—he's safe and sound."

Marie looked at Godpapa Drosselmeier. "Godpapa Drosselmeier, how frightening you looked on top of the clock! Promise you will never do that again." Drosselmeier began to make strange faces, and chanted, in a rasping, monotonous voice, "Pendulums just had to whirr—tick—must whirr gently—whirr—chimes strike loud—boing! boing! and bang and bong! Dolly maid, don't be afraid, for the time is very near to drive the King of Mice away from here. You see, tonight, the owl will come in rapid flight. Tick and tock! Tock and tick! Chimes, ting, ting. Clocks, whirr, whirr, rattle and whirr, prr, prrr!"

Everyone was astonished. "That's the strangest thing I've ever heard," said Fritz. "Haven't you ever heard my clockmaker's song?" replied Godpapa Drosselmeier. "I'm sure you have." But no one could remember having heard it.

He quickly sat down next to Marie. "But here's something more important." He reached into the pocket of his overcoat and pulled out Nutcracker, whose teeth he had mended. "If you're interested, I'll tell you the story of Princess Pirlipat, the witch Mouserink and the crafty clockmaker, and why it is that nutcrackers are so ugly."

Marie perked up, as did Dr. and Mrs. Stahlbaum and Fritz. Godpapa cleared his throat and began:

The Tale of the Hard Nut

Pirlipat's mother was the wife of a king—that is to say, a queen—so that, from the moment she was born, Pirlipat was a princess. The king danced with joy when he saw his little daughter lying in her cradle. Not only was she extremely beautiful, with her delicate complexion, blue eyes and glossy blond hair, but she had been born with all her teeth, like little pearls, as the Lord Chamberlain had learned when she bit him.

But the whole court was nervous about the Princess' well-being. Her cradle was always surrounded by six nurses keeping guard. Each nurse had a cat on her lap, which she stroked constantly, all night long, so that the room was always filled with the sound of purring cats.

Why were these steps taken?

Once, some time before, the King had held a festival at court. Kings and princes from all over the world had come to attend balls, tournaments and grand theatrical presentations. The event was so special that the King decided that, for a feast, the Queen would make her sausages, for which she was famous throughout the kingdom.

The kitchen had been made ready. The Queen put on her damask apron and went to the great golden kettle to begin work. Soon she came to the most important step—cutting bits of fat into little squares that were to be browned over the fire on silver spits. She had just put the spits over the fire when she heard a little voice. "Pray, sister, give me some of the fat. Come, share it with a sister queen." The Queen recognized that voice. It belonged to Dame Mouserink, who had lived in the palace for many years and claimed to be of royal blood. Although she did not regard Dame Mouserink as a queen, the Queen was a kindhearted woman and gave her some of the fat to eat. Then Dame Mouserink's kith and kin came pouring out of the walls, each one demanding some of the tasty fat.

Just in time, the Mistress of the Robes came in and drove the mice away. Some fat was left, which the Queen carefully divided between the sausages, hoping that no one would notice the difference.

When the time came for the sausages to be served, silver kettledrums and trumpets announced the feast. The King, followed by potentates, princes and the entire court, entered the banqueting hall and made ready for the meal. The King's eyes opened wide when the steaming sausages were placed before him on a golden plate. He took a bite. He turned pale. He raised his eyes toward heaven. His breast heaved with sighs. Finally, he held both hands before his face and sank into his seat, sobbing and moaning. "Too little fat!" he gasped.

The Queen rushed in and threw herself at his feet. "Oh, my poor royal husband," she cried. "I am to blame, for I shared the fat with Dame Mouserink and her seven sons and many relations. Oh, it's my fault . . . " The Queen fainted. The King jumped up and called all his ministers together, and they called for the court clockmaker, whose name was the same as my own—Christian Elias Drosselmeier. He was given the task of ridding the palace of the hated mice forever.

Drosselmeier was clever, and invented an ingenious machine into which bits of browned fat were placed to lure the mice. The traps were placed all about the kitchen. Soon Dame Mouserink's seven sons, along with most of her aunts, uncles, nephews, nieces and cousins were trapped and put to a miserable death. But Dame Mouserink was too crafty to be caught, and hatred filled her. One day, she crept behind the Queen and hissed in her ear, "My relatives and sons are no more. Have a care, my lady, lest the queen of the mice bite your princess in two. Have a care!"

And that is why Princess Pirlipat was surrounded by the six nurses with the six purring cats.

The precaution was in vain, for one evening, just at midnight, the chief nurse, sitting next to the cradle, dozed off and woke to find that the whole room—cats and nurses alike—had fallen asleep. Looking at the cradle, she saw, to her horror, that Dame Mouserink was standing on her hind legs, her face pressed against Pirlipat's. The nurse gave a terrified shriek, and Dame Mouserink fled. The noise woke Pirlipat, who began to cry.

"Thank heaven, she is safe!" sighed all the nurses. But their thanks turned to wails and laments when they looked at Pirlipat and discovered what the once lovely child had become. In place of the rosy face of an angel, framed by gleaming golden hair, there was an enormous bloated head on top of a tiny, crumpled body and, where once her beautiful eyes had gleamed, there stared green, wooden-looking eyes. Her mouth stretched from ear to ear. The castle echoed with sobs and wails. The Queen fainted and the King banged his head against the wall.

Drosselmeier was called for at once. Carefully, he took the Princess apart and put her back together again. Shaking his head, he told the King that her condition would only get worse.

"Christian Elias Drosselmeier," roared the King, "cure the Princess or be put to death!"

Drosselmeier began to weep bitterly, but then he noticed that the Princess, who had also been weeping, had taken a nut, cracked it between her huge jaws, and was quietly eating the kernel. In fact, the only way the Princess could be kept happy was by supplying her with nuts to crack. "O mighty Nature!" exclaimed Drosselmeier. "You have shown me the way to solve the problem." He called his dear friend, the court astronomer, and the two went deep into discussion and reading and checking charts until they were ready to draw up Princess Pirlipat's horoscope. The work was hard and long, but when they had finished—oh, joy!—they had the answer they needed: The Princess could be delivered from the spell only by eating the kernel of the nut Crackatook.

The nut Crackatook, it seemed, had a shell so hard that a cannon fired at it could not break it. Moreover, the nut had to be broken in the Princess' presence by the jaws of a young man who had never shaven and had never worn boots.

Drosselmeier and the astronomer hurried to the King to tell him of their discovery. The King embraced Drosselmeier and promised him wonderful rewards for his fine work. "Let's get the job done first thing after dinner," he said. Drosselmeier turned pale, and stammered that, though the remedy for the Princess' condition was known, neither he nor the astronomer had any idea where the nut Crackatook or the young man who was to break it were to be found. Furious, the King waved his scepter over his crowned head and boomed at poor Drosselmeier, "Very well, then . . . off with your head!" But the Queen begged him to spare Drosselmeier's life, and he had eaten a tasty dinner, so he told him that he would be spared if he and the astronomer went off to find the nut and the young man. And the two men set off.

For fifteen years, Drosselmeier and the astronomer wandered in their attempt to find the nut Crackatook and the mysterious man, and in that time so many marvelous adventures happened to them that it would take me four weeks to tell you of them. But their search met with no success, and one day they found themselves in the middle of a great forest in Asia. There Drosselmeier lit his pipe and was suddenly overcome by a terrible homesickness for his native town of Nuremberg. "O Nuremberg, Nuremberg, beloved

native town of world-famous beauty and greatest renown! For one whom the blessing may not befall of living securely within your stout wall, though he's traveled to London, or even Paree, he knows they are nothing contrasted with thee. O Nuremberg, Nuremberg, beloved native town, where houses have windows both upstairs and down." Drosselmeier and the astronomer both began to howl so loudly that they were heard all across Asia.

The two decided that they might just as well hunt for the nut Crackatook in Nuremberg as anywhere else, so they crossed Asia to Germany and found themselves in that city, at the shop of Drosselmeier's cousin, Christoph Zacharias Drosselmeier, a maker of dolls and toys, to whom they told the story of Princess Pirlipat, Dame Mouserink and the nut Crackatook. Christoph Zacharias clapped his hands and cried out in astonishment, "Cousin, cousin, how marvelous! For, unless I am much mistaken, I myself have this nut Crackatook!" He went on to explain that, some years before, a nut vendor had put down his sack of nuts in front of Drosselmeier's shop, gotten into a fight on the street and run away. A wagon, riding over the sack, had smashed all the nuts, save one, which was too hard. This, Drosselmeier had gilded. He was sure it was the nut Crackatook.

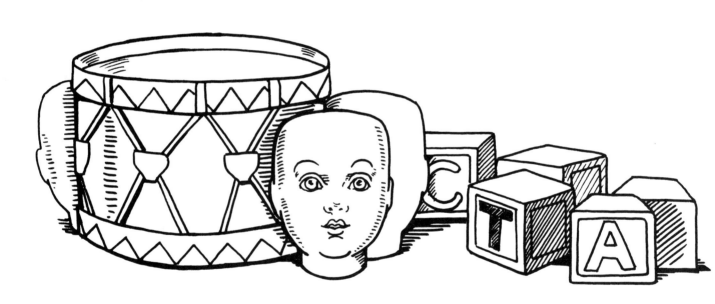

Now all Christian Elias Drosselmeier and the astronomer needed was the young man to crack the nut. The astronomer felt that he too was to be found in Nuremberg—that he was, in fact, Christoph Zacharias Drosselmeier's son—and, casting the young man's horoscope, found out that it was indeed he. They formed a plan. They would take the young man (who, in his younger years, had been a Jumping Jack at Christmas) back to the court, but first they would construct a strong pigtail that would help lever his jaw, so that he would have no trouble in cracking the nut. Then they would let several other young men try to break the nut and, since they would fail, the King would offer the hand of Pirlipat as a reward, which the young Drosselmeier would win.

When they returned to court, and had presented the nut Crackatook to the King, they saw young hopeful after young hopeful go before Princess Pirlipat (who had become even more horrible to look at, having grown a wispy white beard) to crack the nut. All failed. One by one they broke their teeth on Crackatook and had to be led away by the army of dentists who had been assembled. "Goodness," each one sighed, "that was a hard nut."

The young Drosselmeier was presented, made a fine bow, took the nut between his teeth and—CRACK, CRACK!—shattered the shell. Taking the kernel, he gave it to the Princess, who ate it and—oh, wonder!—her beauty returned instantly. The whole court began to dance. The Queen fainted from happiness.

Young Drosselmeier was backing away from the Princess, bowing, just as Dame Mouserink popped up through the floor. The young man stepped on her and, at that very instant—oh, horror!—he was transformed, just as the Princess had been. His body became shriveled and his head huge, with great staring eyes and wide-gaping mouth. Where his pigtail had been there was now a wooden cloak, which controlled the movements of his lower jaw.

In stepping back, he had crushed Dame Mouserink, who lay squeaking on the floor. "O Crackatook, I'm cracked like you. My life is over, oh, boo-hoo! But little Nutcracker, have a care, for though I die, my son will dare, with seven heads, each with a crown, to avenge his mother and bring you down to meet your end! My fate is bleak. I feel myself going . . . gug, gargle, squeak!"

So died Dame Mouserink.

Princess Pirlipat and her father the King both decided that young Drosselmeier, in his new form, was much too ugly for her to marry, and the Lord Chamberlain unceremoniously threw him out the door. Drosselmeier and the astronomer were banished, and were so puzzled that they cast a new horoscope, which foretold that the young Mr. Drosselmeier would remain a nutcracker until he killed the seven-headed King of the Mice and found a lady who was able to love him, ugly as he might be.

"And that, my dear Marie," Godpapa Drosselmeier concluded his long tale, "is why people often say, 'That was a hard nut to crack,' and why nutcrackers are so ugly."

Marie had to spend a week in bed. When she was finally allowed to move about the house, she went to the cupboard to make sure her toys were all right. There, on the shelf, with all his new teeth, was Nutcracker. Remembering Godpapa Drosselmeier's story of Pirlipat and Dame Mouserink, she realized that this Nutcracker was none other than the young Mr. Drosselmeier. Marie looked at Nutcracker. "But why didn't your uncle help you?" she sighed. Then Marie thought she heard, soft as a whisper, a little voice come from the cupboard, "Marie—my angel—be mine."

In the late afternoon, Godpapa Drosselmeier came for tea with the whole family. Marie sat next to him on her little stool and, looking at him for a long time, asked, very seriously, "Godpapa, I know that Nutcracker is your nephew, the young Mr. Drosselmeier from Nuremberg, and that he is a king, or prince, and must destroy the seven-headed King of the Mice in battle. Why don't you help him?"

The family thought that very strange. Dr. Stahlbaum could only shake his head and say, "Child, what has filled your head with such fancies?" But Godpapa Drosselmeier smiled and took Marie onto his lap. "My dear," he said to her, "more is given to you than to any of us, for you, like Pirlipat, are a born princess and rule a shining kingdom. But you will have to go through much for the sake of the Nutcracker, if you want him as your friend, for the King of the Mice awaits him at every corner. I cannot help him—only you can. So be faithful and true to him."

One bright moonlit night not long after, Marie was wakened by a rattling noise that seemed to come from a corner of her bedroom. Then she heard squeaks. "The mice! The mice!" Marie thought to herself, in a near panic. She wanted to run to her mother, but she could not move, for she saw the King of the Mice working himself through a hole in the wall. Finally he entered the room and, with glistening eyes and flashing crowns, climbed a little table that stood next to Marie's bed. "Hee, hee, give me your candy, your marzipan, your candy canes, or I'll eat Nutcracker in the cupboard," he hissed in her ear. He disappeared, going back through the hole in the wall.

The next day, sorrowfully, Marie took her candy and placed it at the bottom of the cupboard. The morning after, Mrs. Stahlbaum said to her, "Isn't it terrible—the mice have gotten into the drawing room, where they have never been before, and have eaten all your nice candies." Marie went in and saw that it was so.

That night, the King of the Mice again entered Marie's room, and hissed in her ear, "Give me your sugar toys, or I'll chew Nutcracker into dust!" Again, Marie went to the cupboard in the morning. This time she was very sad, for she loved the little figures made of sugar—a shepherd and shepherdess with their flock, postmen with letters in their hands, dancers and elegantly dressed couples. In the corner was Marie's favorite, a little baby with red cheeks. Tears sprang into Marie's eyes, for she loved the sugar figures very much. "Oh, dearest Nutcracker, I will do anything to save you, but it is so hard on me!" Weeping, she kissed the sugar figures farewell and put them where the King of the Mice could get at them.

Of course, the King of the Mice ate them all. Mrs. Stahlbaum was very annoyed and thought about getting a cat, but decided that the cat would probably cause as much damage as the mice. Then Fritz suggested that a trap be set. "After all," he said, "if we are to believe the story, it was Godpapa Drosselmeier who invented traps." Everyone laughed, and thought it was a good idea. So a trap was baited and set in the cupboard.

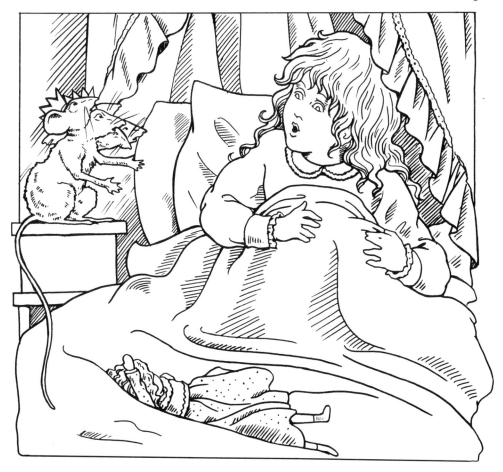

But that night the King of the Mice crept up on Marie's bed and hissed in her ear, "I won't go near the house, it's death for a mouse to nibble the trap's sweetmeat; it's not safe at all to eat. Now give me your picture books, or else I'll get my hooks on Nutcracker, whom I'll bite till he vanishes from sight."

This was more than Marie could stand. She took Nutcracker from his shelf (she had been reluctant to handle him since she had discovered that he was Godpapa Drosselmeier's nephew) and sobbed, "Oh, my dear Mr. Drosselmeier, what can I, poor, unfortunate child, do for you? I am willing to give the evil King of the Mice my beautiful picture books. But I know that he will not be satisfied with them . . . soon I'll have nothing left and he will want to eat *me*! What can I do? What can I do?" As she began to put him back on his shelf, his jaw began to move back and forth, and he said, in a very low voice and with some difficulty, "Ah, dear Miss Stahlbaum, I thank you for everything you have done, but pray, do not give your picture books to the King of the Mice. Give me a sword . . . that is what I need. Then I will be able to deal with him!" And, once again, his eyes became staring and lifeless.

At first, Marie had no idea of where she could get a sword for Nutcracker. Then she turned to her brother for aid, and Fritz took one of the little swords that belonged to a toy soldier of his.

Marie went to bed late that night, but could not sleep. At about midnight she thought she heard a shrill "Squeak!" And then silence. Soon there was a soft knock at the door and a little voice called out, "Good news, Miss Stahlbaum. Please open the door." Marie threw on a robe and ran to open the door. There stood Nutcracker, a bloody sword in one hand, a candle in the other. He knelt before her. "Fear no more, for I have slain the wicked King of the Mice. See, here are his seven crowns, and they are all yours." He took the crowns, which he had placed over his left arm, and gave them to Marie.

"And now, dear Miss Stahlbaum, if you follow me, I will show you delights beyond your imagination." Marie agreed, but told Nutcracker that they must not be gone very long or go very far.

Nutcracker led Marie to the big wardrobe in which Dr. Stahlbaum's traveling cloak, trimmed in fur, hung. Nutcracker gave one of the tassels a pull, and a ladder came through an armhole. When the two climbed the

ladder they found themselves in a dazzling meadow, in which millions of sparks glittered like gems. The air was scented with orange perfume. Nutcracker and Marie moved on to a place called the Christmas Wood, where the leaves on the trees were gold and silver, twinkling in the light and making music as the wind rustled through them. "It's so lovely!" exclaimed Marie. "Can we stay a little longer?"

Nutcracker clapped his hands, and little shepherds and shepherd-
esses, so white and delicate that they might have been made of sugar,
came to dance for Marie's enjoyment. They vanished back into the wood
when their ballet was over, and Nutcracker and Marie went on to the
banks of the Lemonade River. Walking along it, they passed little farms
and the towns of Gingerthorpe and Bonbonville. Finally, they came to the
shores of Lake Rosa, where fish, glistening like diamonds, danced on the
rosy ripples. At the shore, Nutcracker clapped his hands, and from the
distance there came a vehicle, shaped like a shell and covered with gold and
jewels, that was carried above the water by twelve little boys wearing
headdresses and cloaks made of hummingbirds' feathers. Carried above
the water, Nutcracker and Marie were whisked across Lake Rosa,
through gleaming rainbows. Looking into the water, Marie saw the face
of a beautiful princess smiling at her. "See, it's Princess Pirlipat," she cried.
"No, dear Miss Stahlbaum," said Nutcracker. "That is your own reflec-
tion."

Marie and Nutcracker reached the shore and, passing through a grove in which the leaves glittered and sparkled, they arrived at the capital. Its splendor is almost impossible to describe. The walls and towers shone with innumerable colors. The houses, with golden domes instead of roofs, were like nothing else on Earth. The gateway through which Marie and Nutcracker passed was made of macaroons and glazed fruits. Silver soldiers standing sentry cried out, "Welcome, dear Prince! Welcome to Candytown!"

Marie and Nutcracker went on, until they reached the main square. In the center stood a tall cake shaped like an obelisk, from which fountains poured lemonade. There were thousands of people bustling about, making a great uproar. There were ladies and gentlemen, and foreigners in all sorts of clothing, and shepherds and soldiers—in fact, every kind of person there is to be found.

The noise of the crowd grew louder as the Great Mogul entered the square in a litter, followed by ninety-three nobles and seven hundred slaves. By chance, at the same time seven hundred members of the Fishermen's Guild were having a celebration in the square and the Grand Turk was also passing through, attended by several thousand Janissaries,

who ran into the procession of the Great Interrupted Sacrifice, in which a crowd, attended by a full orchestra and chorus, marched toward the obelisk, singing, "Up, up, offer thanks to the Sun!" The noise, the tumult, were terrible indeed. There was pushing and shoving, and soon one of the fishermen accidentally knocked a Brahman's head off. As the fighting spread, a man climbed to the top of the obelisk with a bell, which he rang three times, calling out, "Pastry cook, pastry cook, pastry cook!" Hearing that name, which stood for an unknown and terrible power, the throng at once fell silent. The Brahman's head was stuck back on his shoulders and everyone went about his own business.

Marie and Nutcracker arrived at the Marzipan Castle, the walls of which were covered with bouquets of flowers. The roofs were set with thousands of sparkling gold and silver stars. At the door, they were met by twelve pages who led them inside. Four tiny princesses of the royal blood came out and embraced Nutcracker, calling him "dearest Prince" and "beloved brother." Nutcracker introduced Marie to them. The princesses admired Marie's beauty, each one observing that she was more beautiful by far than Princess Pirlipat.

The princesses led the couple into a room of crystal, filled with precious furniture. They began to prepare a banquet to honor Marie and Nutcracker, and Marie insisted on helping them make the pies and cakes. As she worked, Nutcracker related at length the tale of the King of the Mice. And as he spoke, the sound of his voice and his appearance grew more and more indistinct, and a silvery mist rose up, and Marie felt herself rising, as though on waves, higher and higher until . . .

Thump! Marie fell from a great height.

And, opening her eyes, she found herself in her little bed at home. It was bright day. Her mother, who was standing next to the bed, said, "How long you've been sleeping! Your breakfast has been ready for quite a while." Marie told her mother of her adventure, but her mother told her it was only a beautiful dream that she must put out of her head.

No one believed Marie's story. Dr. Stahlbaum and Fritz laughed at her. But when she showed them the seven tiny crowns of the King of the Mice, which Nutcracker had given her, everyone was amazed. At just that moment, Godpapa Drosselmeier stuck his head in at the door and asked what the commotion was about. He laughed when he saw the seven crowns. "Silly things," he said, "Don't you remember these crowns? I gave them to Marie as a birthday present when she was two." Both Dr. and Mrs. Stahlbaum thought hard and said yes, perhaps they did remember. They told Marie to be less wild with her imagination, or they would throw all her dolls and toys away, and left the matter at that.

But Marie could not forget her marvelous adventures, or her beloved Nutcracker.

One day, not long after, Marie was in the drawing room while Godpapa Drosselmeier repaired one of the clocks. Standing on a stool to look in the cupboard, she saw Nutcracker on his shelf and sighed, "Oh, dear young Mr. Drosselmeier, if you were alive, I would not behave like Princess Pirlipat and reject you because of your ugliness." Godpapa Drosselmeier overheard her and snorted, "Stuff and nonsense!" At that moment, there was a bang and a jolt and Marie fell in a faint.

When she awoke, her mother was next to her and said, "Marie, you must be more careful. See how you fell off the stool." Godpapa Drosselmeier was there too, in his yellow coat and glass wig, and with him was a very handsome young man whom he introduced as his nephew from Nuremberg. He was beautifully dressed, with a little jeweled sword, and he had a magnificent pigtail hanging down his back. He had brought with him little sugar dolls like those of Marie's that the King of the Mice had eaten. He amused the whole family by cracking nuts at the table. Taking a nut and placing it between his jaws, he would tug at his pigtail and—CRACK!—the nut would break, exposing the sweet kernel.

"Play nicely, children," said Godpapa Drosselmeier as he left the two alone. Young Mr. Drosselmeier led Marie to the cupboard and knelt before her. "Oh, dearest Marie," he said. "You see here kneeling before you the very Drosselmeier whom you saved on this spot from the King of the Mice. When you were kind enough to say that you would not be like Pirlipat, and would accept me as I was, immediately I ceased to be an ugly nutcracker and resumed my true appearance. Dame Mouserink's spell is broken. Come with me, be my bride and dwell with me in Marzipan Castle."

Smiling, Marie raised him to his feet. "Dearest Mr. Drosselmeier, how can I refuse a person as good as you are? I would love to rule with you that delightful country and its charming people. I accept your offer."

After a year's engagement, Marie was taken away in a gold coach drawn by silver horses. At the wedding, twenty-two thousand people danced, shining in diamonds and pearls. To this day Marie lives in the land of shining Christmas forests, marzipan castles and wonderful things of every kind, all of which you can see if you have the eyes to see them with.

And that is the story of Nutcracker and the King of the Mice.